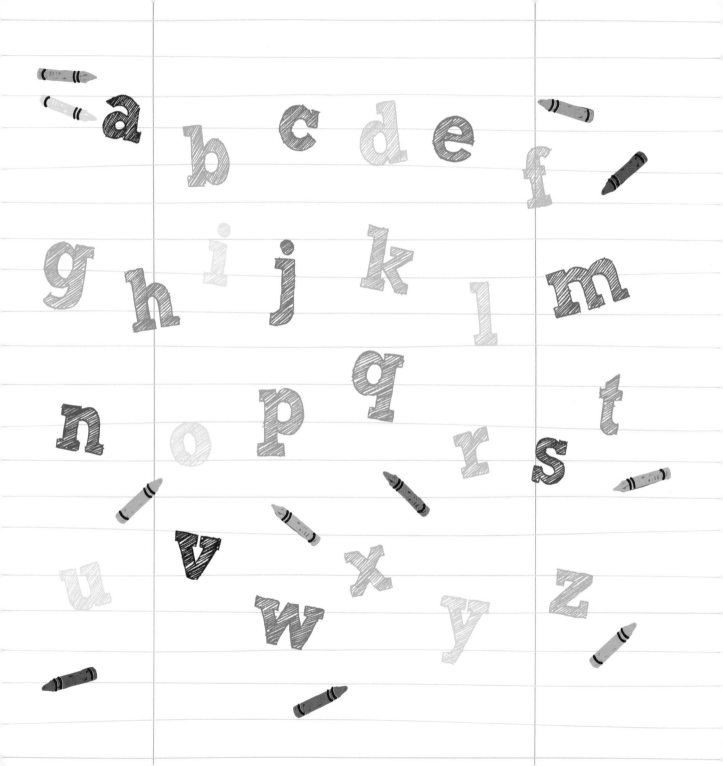

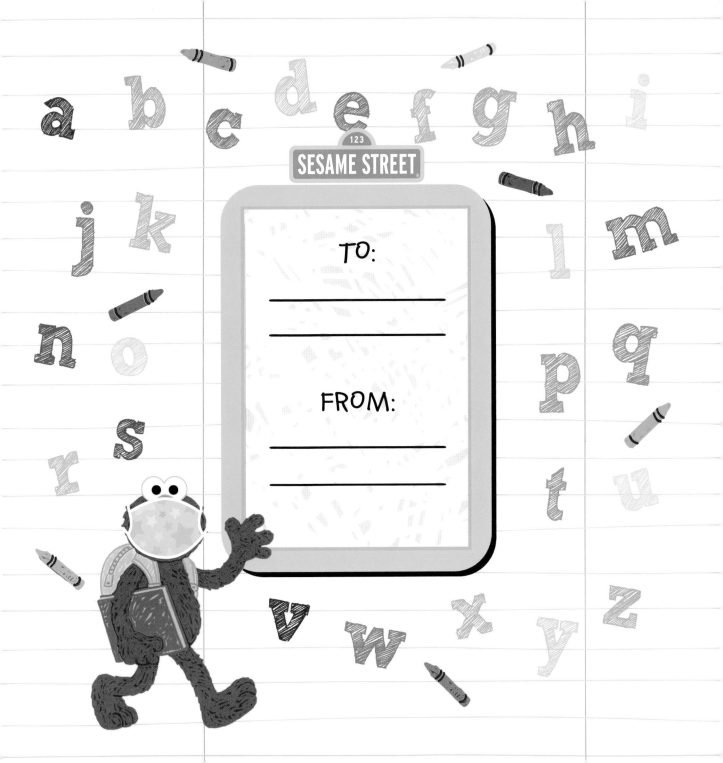

SESAME STREET

TO:

_____

_____

FROM:

_____

_____

This book is dedicated to all the heroic children who wear masks…just like Elmo and friends.

🤍 🤍 🤍   And thank you!   🤍 🤍 🤍

This book would not exist without a world full of helpers. Thank you for keeping all of us safe.

To Sasha & Sawyer—For your copious creativity and ability to always think ahead, thank you.

To all of the Magic Makers—Taylor, Karen, Jordan, Sarah, Michelle, Kelsey, April, Deve, and Jen.
Your dedication and hard work are inspiring. You truly are a dream team!

And to the extraordinary family at Sesame Workshop, thank you for making all of this possible.

Cover and internal design © 2020 by Sourcebooks

Cover illustrations © Sesame Workshop
Internal illustrations by Ernie Kwiat and Joe Mathieu

Sourcebooks and the colophon are registered trademarks of Sourcebooks.

Published by Sourcebooks Wonderland, an imprint of Sourcebooks Kids.
P.O. Box 4410, Naperville, Illinois 60567–4410
(630) 961-3900
sourcebookskids.com

Source of Production: Worzalla, Stevens Point, Wisconsin, USA
Date of Production: August 2020
Run Number: 5019650

Printed and bound in the United States of America.
WOZ 10 9 8 7 6 5 4 3 2 1

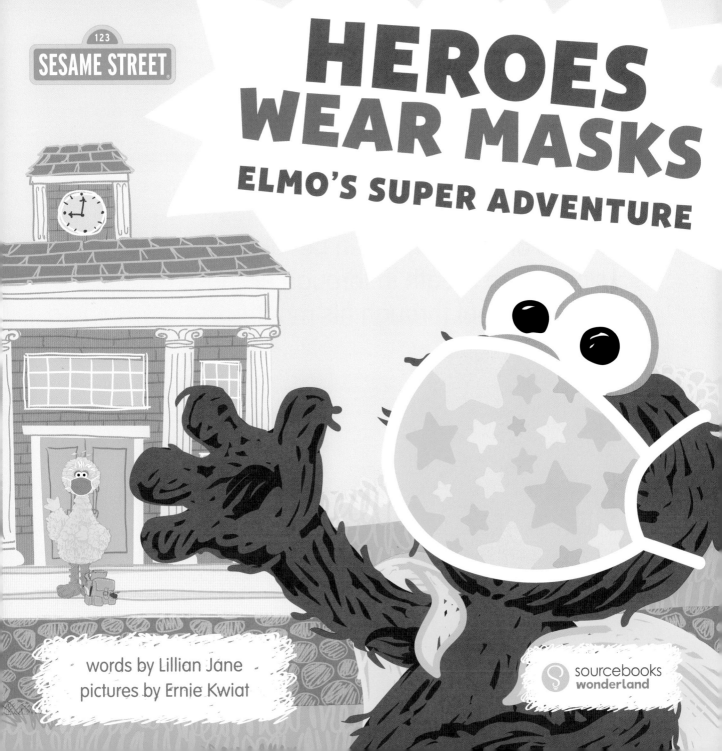

HEROES WEAR MASKS
ELMO'S SUPER ADVENTURE

SESAME STREET

words by Lillian Jane
pictures by Ernie Kwiat

sourcebooks
wonderland

Today, Elmo is going to school!

Elmo is super excited—and super nervous! To feel better, he puts his hands on his belly. Then he takes a slow, deep breath in through his nose and lets it out through his mouth.

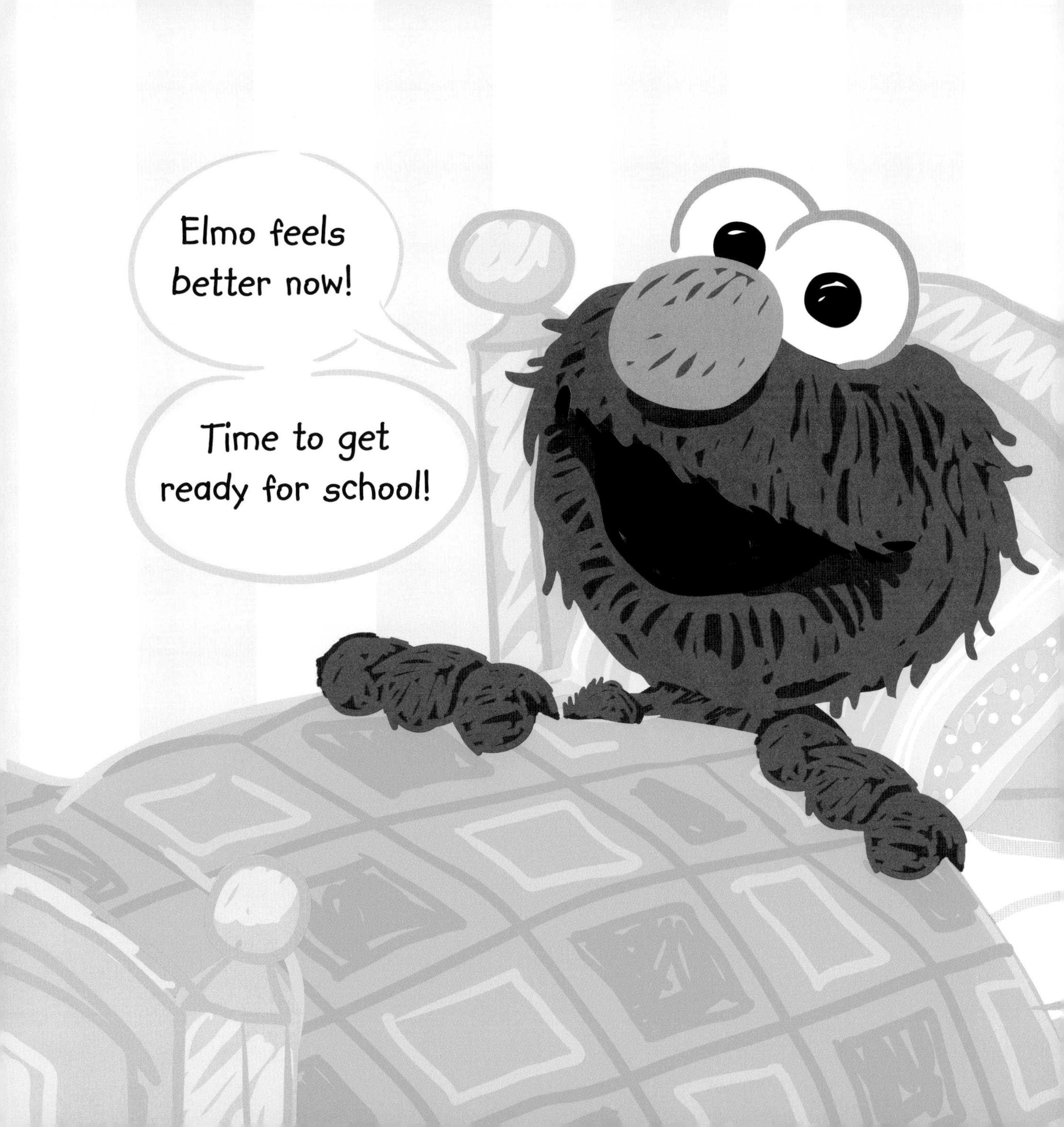
Elmo feels better now!
Time to get ready for school!

First, Elmo washes his hands. Mommy says handwashing is super important!

Wash your hands to the ABC song!

Elmo wets his hands and uses soap to make lots of bubbles. He scrubs for 20 seconds, then rinses and dries his hands.

Elmo eats a healthy breakfast. He wants to have lots of super strength to learn and play. Elmo's mommy tells him what to expect at school today.

First, you may have your temperature taken. And you'll need to wear your mask, keep a safe distance from your friends, and give them big waves but no hugs. OK, Elmo?

Yes, Mommy. And Elmo remembers he shouldn't touch his nose, eyes, or mouth after he washes his hands!

Uh-oh. Elmo still feels nervous about going to school. It's been a while since he has seen his friends.

Elmo takes another belly breath to help himself feel better.

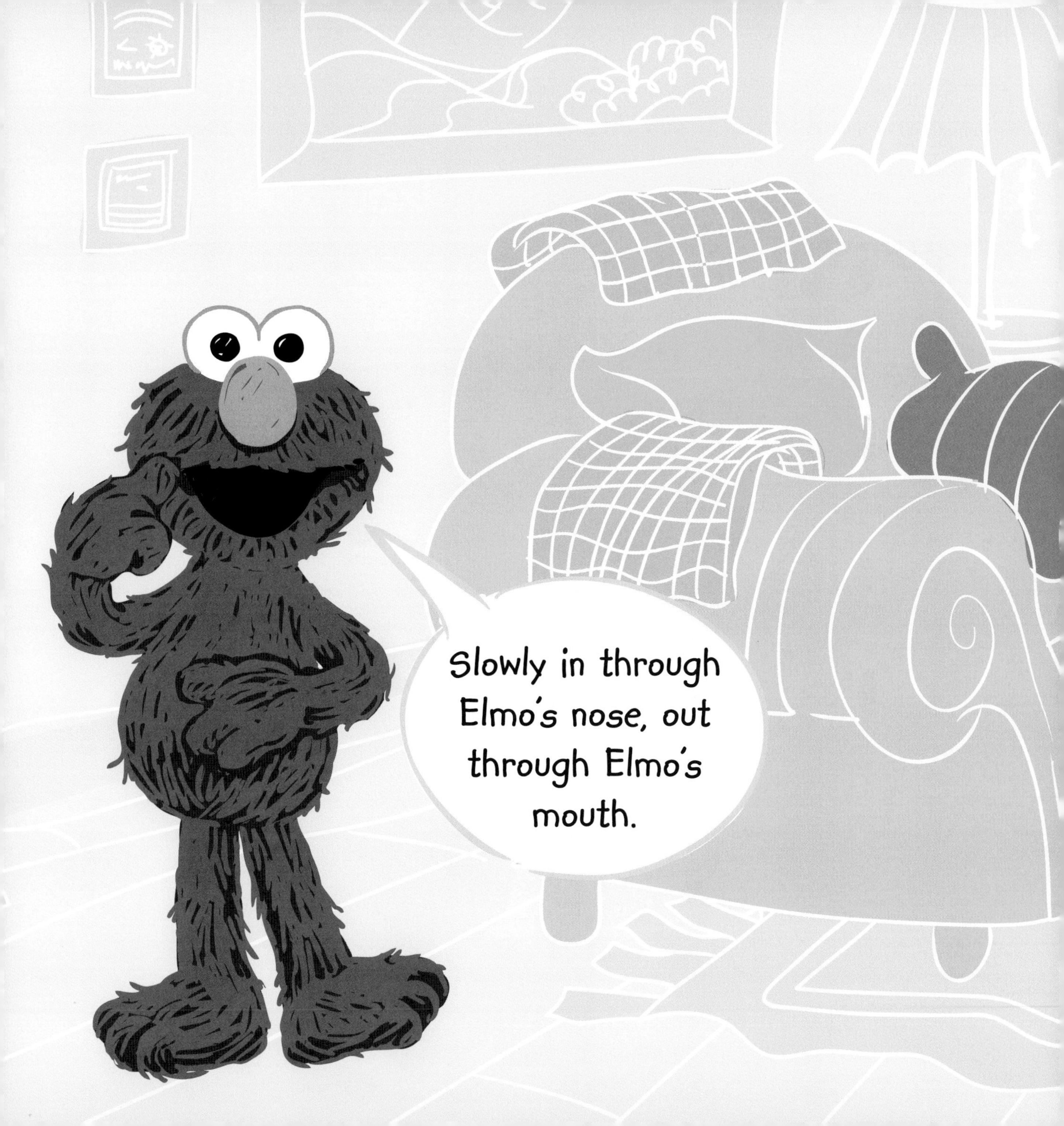
Slowly in through Elmo's nose, out through Elmo's mouth.

Elmo and Mommy pack Elmo's backpack with everything he needs.

Elmo has a face mask to wear at school and whenever he leaves home. Mommy says that wearing a mask is important because it keeps everyone healthy.

Elmo wants to be super ready for school!

Mommy says that a mask should be clean and cover both your nose and your mouth.

Let's try on the mask!

Elmo doesn't wear his mask when he does school work at home, though! Mommy says Elmo only has to wear it when he goes out.

Mommy says even Super Grover wears one because heroes wear masks to keep others safe! All of Elmo's friends will be wearing masks at school too!

Elmo wears a mask just like this! He wants to be a hero too. What does your mask look like?

It's time to leave and walk
to the bus, but Elmo is
getting nervous again.
He knows just what to do.

Elmo puts his hands on his belly, takes a slow, deep breath in through his nose, and lets it slowly out of his mouth. Now he's ready to go!

Elmo asks Mommy where his friends are. Mommy says Elmo's friends will get to school differently.

Some ride the bus, some walk, and some go in cars!

SCHOOL BUS

Remember you can give Mommy a hug and kiss but you have to wave to your friends!

Elmo practices his best wave for Mommy as he says goodbye.

Elmo is nervous about leaving home but also excited to go to school!

When the bus arrives at school, Elmo and his friends line up at a safe distance from each other. Elmo remembers what his mommy told him and gives his friends BIG waves.

Elmo is excited to be with his friends, even if they have to sit far apart. School is going to be so much fun!

Elmo has a very busy—and very fun—day at school!

Elmo knows to wash Elmo's hands when he gets back inside!

After school, Elmo meets Mommy at the bus stop.

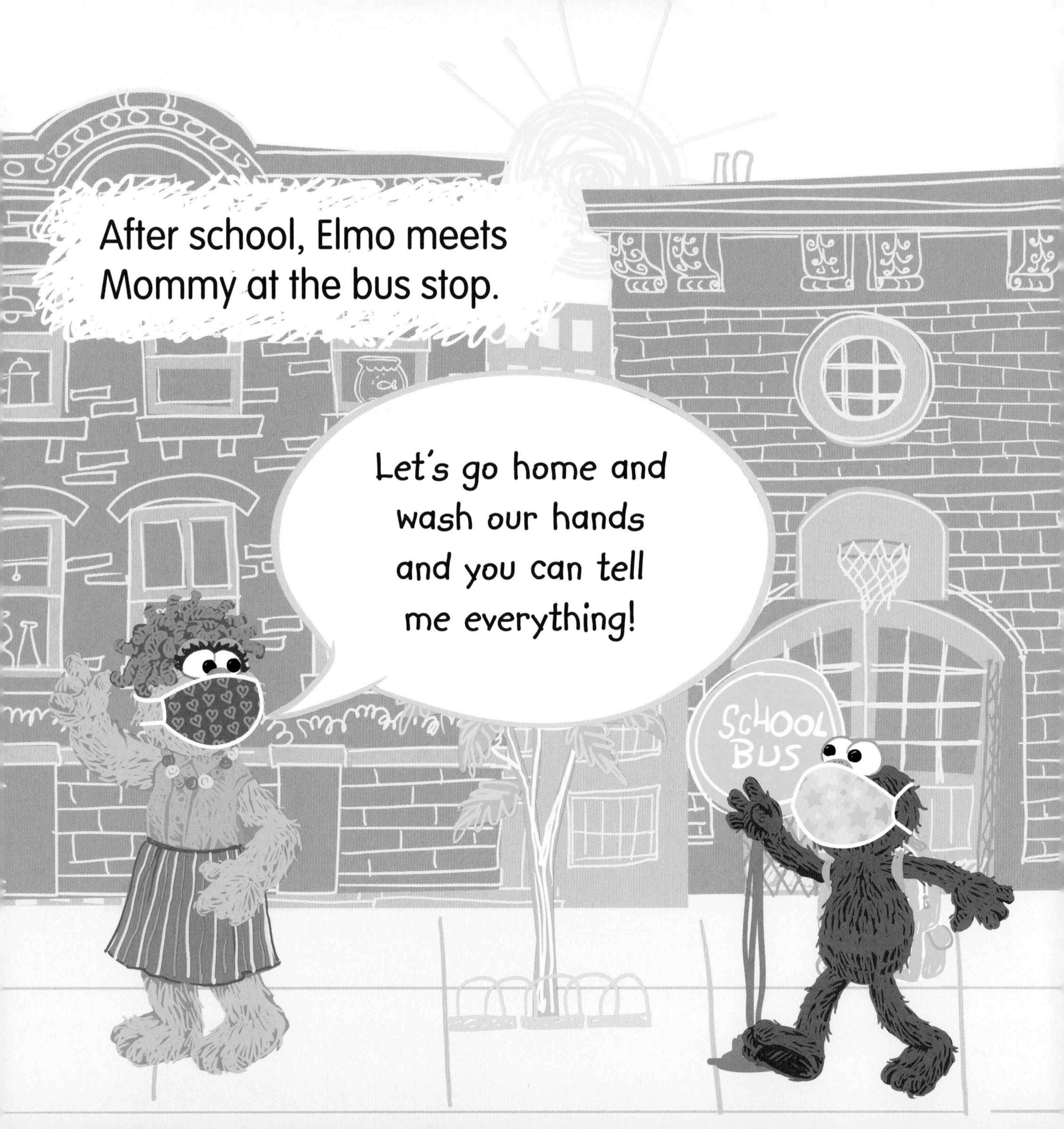

TIPS FOR GROWN-UPS

Do's and Don'ts for Wearing SUPER Face Masks

Help children understand why it's important to wear masks and practice feeling comfortable wearing them.

DO make sure you can breathe through it

DO make sure it covers your nose and mouth

DO make sure that it's clean

DO wear it whenever you go out in public

DON'T play with your mask or touch your face while you're wearing it

DON'T use with children under two years old, unless recommended by your doctor

Germs can make us sick. They're too small to see, but we could carry them in our bodies. You can spread germs even if you feel healthy. Wearing masks and washing your hands keeps others safe from germs we may have.

How to Wash Your Hands

It's important to wash your hands frequently and keep reminding kids to wash before eating, after going potty, and after playing outside. It helps when children see their family or caregivers wash their hands.

STEP 1: Wet your hands with water.

STEP 2: Use soap and scrub your hands together for 20 seconds.

You can sing the ABC song twice. Make lots of suds!

STEP 3: Rinse your hands with water.

STEP 4: Dry your hands with a clean towel.

Other Ideas for Staying Healthy

MOVE AROUND! Exercise can help us feel better and will help us sleep at night. Dancing, stretching, and playing indoor games are fun ways to move your body.

SLEEP! Make sure you get a good night's sleep to stay healthy. Try setting a routine before bed that will help you get to sleep faster.

EAT WELL! Nutritious food is good for your mind and body. Eating healthy food, like a rainbow of fruits and vegetables, helps us stay healthy.

Six feet is the size of Daddy lying down!

PRACTICE STAYING APART TO HELP EVERYONE STAY HEALTHY! Keep six feet away from others when you're out in public and visit places at less crowded times if you do need to go out.

Helping Children with School Anxiety

Talk with your child about what they can expect at school.

Practice belly breathing with your child by having them put their hands on their tummies and breathe. Take slow, deep breaths in through the nose, and then release slowly out through the mouth.

Reassure them that you will always be there for them. Have your child carry a photo of a loved one to school, or tie matching strings around their wrist and yours so they can touch it and feel connected to you.